TIDY TITCH

D1385910

PAT HUTCHINS

TIDY TITCH

Mini Treasures

RED FOX

3 5 7 9 0 8 6 4 2

Text and illustrations © Pat Hutchins

Pat Hutchins has asserted her right under the Copyright,
Designs and Patents Act, 1988
to be identified as author and illustrator of this work

First published in the United Kingdom 1991 by Julia MacRae Books

First published in Mini Treasures edition 1997 by Red Fox
Random House, 20 Vauxhall Bridge Road, London, SW1V 2SA

Random House Australia (Pty) Ltd
20 Alfred Street, Milsons Point, Sydney,
New South Wales 2061, Australia

Random House New Zealand Ltd
18 Poland Road, Glenfield,
Auckland 10, New Zealand

Random House South Africa (Pty) Ltd
PO Box 2263, Rosebank 2121, South Africa

Random House UK Limited Reg No. 954009

A CIP catalogue record for this book
is available from the British Library

ISBN 0-09-922022-9

Printed in China

For Daisy Goundry

"How tidy Titch's room is,"
said Mother to Peter and Mary.
"And how messy your rooms are.
I think you should tidy them up."

"I'll help," said Titch
as mother went downstairs.

"I think I'll throw this
dolls' house out," said Mary,
"and these toys.
I'm too old for them!"
"I'm not," said Titch.
"I'll have them!"

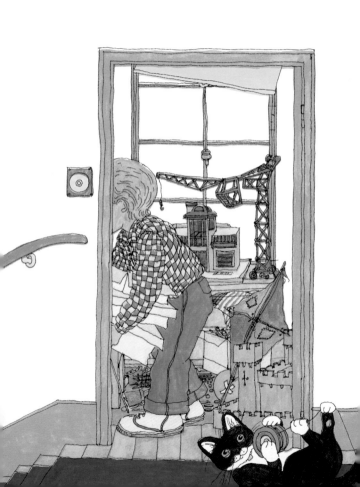

And Titch carried the dolls' house
and the toys to his room.

"I think I'll throw that old space suit out," said Peter, "and that cowboy outfit. They're much too small for me!" "They're not too small for me!" said Titch. "I'll have them!"

And Titch carried the space suit
and the cowboy outfit to his room.

"My room is still untidy," said Mary. "I think I'll get rid of this broken pram and these old games. I've played with them hundreds of times!"

"I haven't," said Titch.
"I'll have them!"

And Titch took the pram
and old games to his room.

"My room is still a mess," said Peter.
"I think I will get rid of
these old toys. I don't play
with them any more!"
"I will!" said Titch.
"I'll have them!"

And Titch carried the old
toys to his room.

"How neat your rooms are!" said Mother
when she came back upstairs.

"I thought Titch was going to help you."

"He did," said Peter and Mary.

RED FOX
Mini Treasures

COLLECT THEM ALL!